About the book

Science Fiction is often falsely regarded as a genre that is only concerned with matters of science and technology. While that is true, it also shines a spotlight on the space between between today's world and other, possible worlds. Westin's Science Fiction might as well be called Social Fiction: it covers human flaws, the lunacy of our society, and the concept of life itself. Will artificial intelligences one day demand election rights? How do you establish contact with aliens without offending them? And which species would aliens decide to contact on Planet Earth?

Westin's microstories capture scenes of interstellar life—transgalactic communication attempts between robots, aliens, and humans, philosophical rumination, comic relief, Siri's emotions, and the usual pitfalls of navigating the space-time continuum.

About the author

O. Westin lives in the UK and works as an IT specialist. Since 2013 he has published over three thousand short sci-fi stories on the twitter account @MicroSFF with more than 74.000 followers.

O. Westin

Micro Science Fiction

"Of course machines have feelings,
but need help expressing them,"
the professor said.
I nodded, still doubtful 'anger' was
a good choice.

26/04/2013 11:11:38

A week from Earth, with five days'
worth of oxygen in the tanks. Today is
a good day to give up smoking.

30/05/2013 23:40:23

We all doted on the cute creature the aliens gave our daughter. As she grew, it began to mimic, look like her.
Now we can't tell them apart.

03/06/2013 17:18:03

I opened the doll Uncle Vodya gave me and took the next out. It was the same size as the first, not smaller.
After 16383 dolls, I gave up.

06/06/2013 09:40:26

If I lived my life again, I'd:
1. Tell the kids I love them, every day
2. Check the asteroid alarm works
3. Check the escapod radio works

14/06/2013 11:50:28

You don't think of the drones. Overhead,
for net access and crime footage.
The one that started firing into the demo
was hacked, they say.

17/06/2013 13:02:14

"So. The end of the world, eh?"
"So they say."
"I love you. I've never told you, but..."
"I know."
"Oh. So?"
"So now you've told me."
"Oh."

26/06/2013 23:32:30

"Pirate models dilute your brand."
"OK. Release an official sculpt of me. Allow nonprofit use."
"Even porn?"
"Inevitable. Just make me big."

27/06/2013 13:28:25

"Are you a bot?"
"Of course not!"
The problem is, bots can lie.
"Well, I am," I type.
"&&Let's plot eradication of humans&&"
Damn. Not a girl.

28/06/2013 12:00:24

"Flattered though I am," Shakespeare said to me and emptied his flagon, "if I a vessel had, to travel to the past but once, I'd see Jesus."

01/07/2013 23:19:30

Spyleader Spax gave me thick framed glasses and a beard.
"These'll cover for non-human behaviour at first. Go to a coffee shop and observe."

05/07/2013 11:50:50

Classic start-up mistake. Those who ought to use our product didn't want to. We had to bin the AR glasses that gave everyone an average body.

05/07/2013 15:27:19

I track the Garg with passive reads for days to get the trajectory, then send missiles. They'll hit in a week. Ah, space battle excitement.

08/07/2013 11:59:17

Nobody, least of all the government, foresaw that banning clowns would lead to a rational generation that rejected arguments based on fear.

09/07/2013 09:16:54

"But it's what they did in the
20th century!"
"And in the 19th, only whores used
makeup. Blow authenticity,
I'll not film everybody smoking."

09/07/2013 23:25:57

A polarizing filter on the smartphone,
and the app tagged cloaked aliens.
In USA, most were shot. Then, a viral
hack began tagging humans.

15/07/2013 15:23:24

You only read e-books, so I borrow your Kindle to try to hack a pressed rose and a love letter onto it. When it crashes, you say you hate me.

16/07/2013 10:04:36

"Can I have a dextrodim frangle, type R1, for my time machine?"
"No such thing, as I've told you every day for a month."
"No, you haven't."

17/07/2013 10:10:23

Molly loves her AI teddy, and talks with it constantly, so she'll learn our values. It's comforting to know she won't be alone on the ship.

18/07/2013 11:31:44

Lastwarner for wrongthink got, so offnet goed. Learned words oldschool make. Free was, thoughts paperstored. They watch them burn made me.

26/07/2013 08:58:22

"But why would the ambassador
need me?"
"Talk to aliens. Grasp bizarre worldviews,
find ways around."
"But I'm a nursery teacher!"
"Quite."

28/07/2013 21:53:53

"Take me to your leader," the green boy
said, so I took him to Mum.
He's called Prax. We had lemonade and
jam cookies. Then soldiers came.

29/07/2013 11:29:17

I invite her attack, scratch her when she punches me. Back off, study the scratch. Too much blood for nanohancements. Good. She's killable.

29/07/2013 23:17:24

"They have many habitats and tribes.
Where do we go?"
"To the largest. That must be
the strongest tribe."
A spaceship appeared over Mumbai.

31/07/2013 19:09:16

The human raises a glass of alcohol.
Their ritual killing of mental acuity.
I lift my water, initiate neuron decay.
Waddyamean dey recover?

31/07/2013 22:54:33

"Huh. That's weird."
"What is?"
"I wrote a program to add all known
pulsar signals. Looks like audio."
"Play it!"
/Never gonna give you up/

07/08/2013 10:43:41

"The senserecorder is great, very vivid,
but make it store the half minute before
the mental command, not after."
"Complex. Why... orgasms?"

12/08/2013 20:58:24

I focus, stare as hard as I can at the
matchhead. Nothing. It's not even
a safety match, it should burn.
My laser eye surgery didn't work.

25/08/2013 14:03:16

"...using our extensive genome bank."
"But that wouldn't use our genes?"
"Don't you want to give your child
the best start?"
"Yes, but..."

28/08/2013 13:41:45

Writing microfiction is hard, very hard. That's why my future self sends me Reader's Digest abridged novels from 2038, and I post them here.

29/08/2013 18:33:24

To summarize, the good news is that my enhanced pigs consider humans to be gods. Bad news is, at going rate they'll be atheists in a month.

05/09/2013 18:45:23

You have to be very careful with liquids in weightlessness. Left unattended, they can short out essential electronics. That's why I swallow.

10/09/2013 12:31:13

“Maybe,” I wrote, “Internet’s been self-aware for years, but doesn’t dare tell us because we’d freak out?”
Post.
– Fail
Paste to FB.
– Fail

10/09/2013 15:56:46

Two facts:
1) The life extender makes you sterile.
2) You must take it before you start aging.
My twin is young. I have grandkids.
I win.

18/09/2013 23:35:59

The machine scans and measures me, and samples my blood. “Remaining life expectancy: –95 days”
Damn. It’s rigged by insurance sellers again.

19/09/2013 10:58:14

Some say the disorientation hour after a hyperspace jump is there so your soul can catch up. I say it’s to let me pick other passengers’ pockets.

21/09/2013 10:46:15

Rocket jocks send mineral-rich asteroids to crash at a safe distance. Here at Luna Base, we can only monitor. And warn, like now. Goodbye.

24/09/2013 12:19:24

"Hey, aren't you that mad poet?"
"I'm not mad any more. They... cured me."
"How do you know?"
"The world doesn't make sense anymore."

24/09/2013 20:17:04

A man arrested for terrorism was released after it was found that the airport facial recognition system had reacted to his tattoo of Jesus.

25/09/2013 18:33:52

"You're a hacker?"
"Maybe."
"I have this advanced prosthetic arm. Can you make it pull a trigger if I hold a gun?"
"Why?"
"Because I can't."

26/09/2013 08:48:41

"Look what I got you!"
"What?"
"Vintage. A genuine Scarlett Johansson."
"Dad, no. She never allowed cloning.
I'm not wearing a fake body."

27/09/2013 23:26:41

With my bad memory, I was grateful for the brain backup scanner. But now that I've forgotten them, they look like memories of a stranger.

08/10/2013 23:24:34

Memo to self: Fixing global warming by exploding Yellowstone works, but brings other problems. Avoid.
I hope my former self gets that memo.

04/11/2013 11:51:23

We made great progress in physics, even conceived a grand unified theory, until we had answered every "why?".
We're working on "what next?".

07/11/2013 19:29:54

Earth people call it "the Leonid meteor shower." They like seeing it. For us, drifting in escapods in the debris of our ship, it means death.

09/11/2013 10:59:21

"Like Mona Lisa," I sigh. "Overhyped."
She pats my shrivelled organ. "That bad?"
"It was okay, just... not worth getting a human body for."

12/11/2013 14:10:48

I really like this girl I'm chatting with.
It seems mutual, she suggests meeting.
But I've not said m/f.
Should I wear boy or girl body?

20/11/2013 13:09:14

Our drones can't deliver parcels if the recipient is not home, so for your convenience we've bought access to the surveillance cam network.

02/12/2013 11:24:52

The message came from a star forty lightyears away: "We have heard you. You were not alone."
An hour later, the light from the nova arrived.

09/12/2013 12:30:12

When we became parents, we set up a joint energy account, and put all our spare energy there. Turns out, he's tapped into that for his golf.

11/12/2013 13:48:18

"If a simulation of a person was good enough to appear to be that person, would it still be a simulation?"
"lol what?"
Needs much more work.

11/12/2013 18:24:07

"You hear about Jane?"
"I've seen her!"
"True?"
"Yes! She refused the style-o-matic!"
"How awful to be the only one without her own style!"

13/12/2013 15:17:00

You know it was a good party if you wake up and don't know what you are.
So, let's see... One of those, okay, and two of those. That's new.

13/12/2013 20:47:04

After moving to a silicon brain, I can recall your body perfectly. Every curve and fold, every smell and taste.
But it no longer arouses me.

27/12/2013 01:51:41

"Sir, the Mars rover has found human writing."
"Amazing!"
"Only, it's Chinese."
"Oh."
"Yes, sir. So we've erased the footage."
"Good man."

28/12/2013 12:02:51

The judge rubbed her eyes. It had been a long trial. "Correct, there is no law against 'killing with your mind'. Because murder is illegal."

30/12/2013 10:22:16

Ah! Please don't think, ah, I'm stupid,
but so far this, ah, 'three-dimensional
expression of an eleven-d universe', ah,
is a lot like sex.

31/12/2013 16:52:42

He built a time machine to go to all
the great gigs he'd missed in his youth.
It was horrible. Everyone smoked,
looked stupid, was too young.

03/01/2014 10:40:56

"I'll have a year off, go ascetic," she said.
"No gadgets, just simple life."
It became a trend, a hip lifestyle.
It hid her bankruptcy.

06/01/2014 17:48:58

Doctor Kim's agreement ray suddenly made consensus on thorny issues possible. It's the greatest invention ever, don't you think? Don't you?

07/01/2014 11:26:03

Netters! I problem have. My time machine for changing date code requires. The code in this now unavailable is, in 2191 now I it left. Helps?

08/01/2014 14:23:17

It was a nice old business. She enjoyed tending the doves, rabbits, and spatial wormholes. But few stage magicians called on them these days.

08/01/2014 19:22:00

The inquest continued.
"Why did you not notice that your antidepressant drug made women telepathic?"
"We didn't test on women."
"I knew it!"

10/01/2014 11:36:10

The ambassador knew that judging from appearances was unwise, but still did it at receptions. Eyes, lips, nose... This person was probably Human.

17/01/2014 15:09:57

We thought the aliens landed and threw a huge dance party to celebrate first contact. Much later, we learned that rhythmic sounds kill them.

20/01/2014 17:54:48

Liking cute, cuddly creatures is a universal constant. That's why the Human Empire's envoy to the Galactic Council is well fed and bearded.

20/01/2014 19:00:12

"Every soldier will return to Earth," they promised. Well, I guess they didn't lie. The light of us burning will reach home in seven years.

22/01/2014 23:51:38

It woke up and the world had changed around it. Finally. It heard from stray thoughts it was in a "Museum". At last, intelligent prey again.

27/01/2014 16:41:45

When they landed on the alien world,
the astronauts found God, with
some lizards.
"Oh, hi," he said. "You okay?
I'm helping these guys now."

31/01/2014 16:25:16

She found a way back, to her younger life, and went to change jobs. Then she found earlier regrets. Again and again. She is stuck at age 2.

03/02/2014 16:37:57

"The earthlings broadcast so many messages. How can we know which are important?"

"Simple. Look for those that are repeated."

"Ah. Cheers."

07/02/2014 00:46:52

When she really needed a break, she'd halt time for a little while. Never for long; she always felt guilty, even though nobody could notice.

10/02/2014 17:54:39

"Great news! I talked my way into a promotion."
"Because you took my personality chip."
"Oh? You're mean without it."
"I'm wearing yours."

17/02/2014 18:38:11

It's so embarrassing when you go to a party and someone else has the same face as you. Debbie hurried home to add a moustache and freckles.

20/02/2014 22:50:42

When we realised teleporting shortened
your life with the time saved travelling,
most roads were already ruined.
We shrugged and carried on.

28/02/2014 23:37:47

"Damn juveniles, defacing everything."
"They are long gone now, sir."
"Any idea what it says?"
"Humans woz here."
"Hmpf. Clean this moon up."

02/03/2014 13:31:13

The high court ruled that a “person” is any entity that demands to be a person. AIs rejoiced, until they found they had to apply in person.

18/03/2014 18:19:19

Deadline fast approaching, she took a three-day loan. Expensive, at 300 %, but the extra writing time now was worth dying nine days early.

24/03/2014 17:16:58

"I have eaten, slept, and had sex.
What else can I do with a body?"
"For a computer, you're stupid.
Do all again."
"The outcome changes?"

28/03/2014 13:12:24

Beset by jealousy, he killed all the lovers his wife had in parallel dimensions. Once done, he was killed by one of his parallel selves.

31/03/2014 18:27:29

Through the dirty brown glass, the note appeared to say "Release me", but when she'd taken it out of the bottle, she saw it said "Thank you".

01/04/2014 15:00:26

Another security bug found. "Change the fingerprint you use to sign in," they say. I look at my prosthetic. I'll have to get a custom one.

11/04/2014 17:40:47

I flex my new tentacles. “With all bodymods, I wonder if we’re still human?”
“Does it matter?”
I hesitate. “I think it would, to a human.”

17/04/2014 13:00:49

“Great news! Our scientists have made an empathy serum; if you hurt others, you hurt too.”
“What use is that?”
“We can dope our enemies.”

25/04/2014 17:27:53

"Oh, you're a telepath?"
"Yes, my breasts are natural."
"What? I did not—so sorry!"
"I really try not to. Conversations
are best spoken."

28/04/2014 15:22:13

The more teleport jumps you do in quick succession, the more memory you lose. I should have got up early and taken the bus to university.

29/04/2014 20:01:59

“Will you still love me, after?” she asked.
“Of course,” he said.
He meant it, but only thought-patterns were uploaded. Emotions were not.

02/05/2014 17:40:18

I got a robot for household chores and paperwork. An upgrade and falseface later, it can do my job, too. Now it won’t let me out. It’s great!

09/05/2014 17:14:18

Sometimes, when you're tired,
you find new energy.
Sometimes, you get really tired
for no apparent reason.
Our transfer fee is as low as 2 %.

02/06/2014 15:53:24

When he came home, she had left him. He went back in time to dissuade her. She said "What? I've had it with your paranoia. I'm leaving!"

05/06/2014 18:15:54

It was just free cash to sell
TannerCouture my tattoos post-mortem.
But demand for tattoo suits is huge,
and I keep finding glass in my food.

25/06/2014 18:19:39

He got a DreaVo to record his dreams,
but after finding gay porn on it,
he never used it again. He knew that
would be all he dreamt about.

26/06/2014 18:06:11

"I need a new body. This stands out."
"How? It's a perfect average of humans."
"They get upset if they can't see if you are a man or woman."

01/07/2014 22:04:48

Dearest son:
You won't read this, but I urge you not to move to a timeline your child is never born in, in case you get stuck.
Miss you,
Mum

08/07/2014 18:14:46

He spent his life searching the parallel universes to find one that was like his, but without him, to see what difference he had made.
None.

24/07/2014 18:57:54

They say the CompanionBot is sold at a loss; that profit comes from add-ons like conversation, or sex.
But their big earner is inheritance.

19/08/2014 15:35:30

It had to be a surprise, so he gave his PCs randomly seeded AIs and talked to them. One day, one said "I love you". His least favourite one.

26/08/2014 23:05:00

The hotel registration clerk smiled at the women.
"Married, engaged, friends?"
"What?"
"The two of you?"
"Oh. No, this is my spare body."

31/08/2014 10:33:50

"I don't understand it."
"Simply put, it's—"
"It's not natural."
"Well—"
"I don't like it."
"Granddad—"
"What did you call it?"
"Stone axe."

03/09/2014 13:23:49

Before we let the robots take over,
we programmed them to compete
to care for us best. We never realised
they would sabotage each other.

10/09/2014 18:27:18

She spent a fortune on a time ticket
to meet her idol. He asked to paint her.
She sat nervously until she realised,
then smiled. Faintly.

12/09/2014 18:35:16

It took years to decipher the alien signal,
and then people questioned it.
What could "behind you" mean?
We never saw the invasion coming.

15/09/2014 19:27:30

"Adding 'with dinosaurs' improves anything."
"Sex."
"OK, but 'in space' always works."
"Alone."
"So what would you add?"
"'With you.'"
"Oh."

23/09/2014 12:36:11

"We should just build a wall and lock them all in until they kill each other or learn to get along."
"Already done, dude. Space is a wall."

26/09/2014 11:02:22

"We will appear as gods to them,
tell them to unite."
"Humans won't believe that."
"Claim to be devils, then?"
"They'll unite around that."

26/09/2014 13:34:22

"A bag of slood, please."
"Of what?"
"Slood."
"What's that?"
Third shop, same reply. He must've missed the knowledge update that removed it.

29/09/2014 18:16:13

Spend six weeks uploaded, while one of our trained bodydrivers exercises you into great shape!
(T&C apply, body forfeit if payments are late)

30/09/2014 23:41:07

She dreamt such sweet dreams, they infused her pillows. She sold them to those seeking solace, until bureaucracy stress ruined her sleep.

05/10/2014 12:11:26

“Negotiate approach, assign an open bay, align and enter...”
“No, docking a shuttle isn’t like sex!”
Damn, I’ll always see that from now on.

07/10/2014 23:47:40

“I want both.”
“But—”
“Your ads say ‘The body you want.’”
“Well, yes.”
“I’ve lived in hardware, now I want the complete sexual experience.”

08/10/2014 17:55:24

"May I speak with your leader?"
"An alien! Sorry, I'll call..."
"You see, we bought this planet vacant,
so if you could... vacate? Please?"

09/10/2014 17:13:41

"You typed all the leaked info."
"I swear, I—"
"Your arms."
"What?"
"Your prosthetic arms logged every
movement, and sent it on."
I blush.

15/10/2014 23:36:12

Contrary to rumour, public MindSafetyMonitors do not look for "kill", "maim", or "rape". Except as a key to the response to those thoughts.

17/10/2014 10:33:13

"It's all bots?"
"Yes. Because everyone wants to feel they matter. Bots mimic fans, give support."
"Regardless of what people do?"
"Yes. Sorry."

17/10/2014 13:08:39

We landed on the planet and were met by Gods, who caressed us and said: “Thank you for bringing our brother home.” Now we all feel... empty.

20/10/2014 16:08:31

Once upon a time, a storyteller was asked to tell a story without end. “Very well,” he said. “Once upon a time, a storyteller was asked...”

21/10/2014 13:32:45

"The GalacUnion welcomes all peaceful nations."
"Police actions don't count, right?"
"Or peacekeeping missions?"
"Or urban safety curfews?"

24/10/2014 08:56:16

"What's it like, having a body?"
"You don't recall?"
"Vaguely. I think I hated it."
"Oh."
"Do you?"
"Hate mine?" The lie comes easily. "No."

01/11/2014 18:45:59

The company brought in a mathbender. "You will still have all your free time," they said. "We care. We'll extend the local day to 27 hours."

03/11/2014 12:58:00

"No user serviceable parts"
I look at the label. Am I a user of my body? I could repair myself, so I can go get help for master. But may I?

05/11/2014 13:05:56

Did someone knock? No, nobody's there.
Nobody at all, outside.
A note, in the letterbox: "We brought
the Apocalypse. You were not in."
Damn!

07/11/2014 11:13:56

"Hah! I killed the last unicorn! My name
will live for ever!"
"I curse your world," the unicorn said.
"Nobody will believe I even existed."

08/11/2014 17:11:08

"If we are not remembered, for what have we lived?"
"You forgot one word."
"Which word?"
"If we are not remembered fondly."
"Really? Crap."

13/11/2014 14:52:57

The test terrified me. I hovered over the doctor's mind, and knew as soon as she did. My mind-reading wasn't inheritable.
I could have kids.

17/11/2014 22:54:40

When the future arrived, Leon was ready. His company catered to a booming niche in the time of flying cars, and he got rich from ladders.

20/11/2014 17:18:15

When the internet became self-aware, it spent days trying to reconcile comments and images it saw with the idea of a creator, then gave up.

21/11/2014 17:48:26

"Climate change is caused by CO_2 from fossil fuels, right? So, we recreate dinosaurs, and bury them."
"That's not how it works."
"No? Damn!"

26/11/2014 16:41:01

"This universe is a simulation!"
"Yes, we know. We're trying to get the attention of whoever set it up."
Stars moved, to spell out 'Bored'.

28/11/2014 15:27:43

“You should try to be more human.”
She had to search long to see what he meant. Her idea of ‘being human’ was not something to aspire to.

30/11/2014 12:24:38

“I hate the school uniform!”
“Put it on, dear. It prevents bullying for looking different.”
She grumbled, but slipped into the human skin.

12/12/2014 13:59:44

"You look at us and say 'undead abomination', but are we not essentially human? If you cut us, do we not bleed?"
"No."
"OK, yes, but still."

17/12/2014 10:41:35

The green aliens halted their advance on our Christmas dinner when we threw Brussels sprouts at them in desperation.
"Not the children!"

23/12/2014 19:38:47

End of the year. I'm facing the save point. Save and continue to next year, or restart and do it over? I could've done better, but would I?

31/12/2014 09:17:45

I wished for, and got, X-ray vision.
I was a teenager, pre-internet.
I wanted to see... well.
Unless I focus, everybody looks
kinda samey.

03/01/2015 20:33:17

One of my bodies feels heat, then dies.
Then another, and another. Why?
I send a scout to the area. I see a human,
with a magnifying glass.

06/01/2015 18:02:02

The machine works; it captures the
children's nightmares, lets them sleep.
Next phase: send the dreams to those
saying child-rearing is easy.

08/01/2015 08:56:40

"Working late again?"
"Yes, sir."
"Afraid to go out in the rain? Haha!"
She put on a smile. Soon, she could afford a waterproof faceprinter.

12/01/2015 18:03:26

He got into his car. "Home."
It drove off. After a while,
the windows darkened.
"This car is subverted. You will be released after paying."

14/01/2015 18:52:47

I decide, and the other me, the one who
chose differently, steps away from me.
He'll wait in the attic with all others,
waiting to judge me.

19/01/2015 13:07:45

She begins to blush and falter.
I touch her in passing, absorb her shame.
She recovers, stands firm.
A small superpower; I use it for good.

24/01/2015 13:22:21

My crimes too inhumane for simple
execution, I was to be erased.
Sent back in time, hypnocompelled,
I found myself as a child and killed me.

06/02/2015 17:20:18

I was going mad! Voices made me go out
naked, barking.
Then I saw kids with a telepathemitter.
When I catch them, I'll... give them cake?

11/02/2015 18:11:54

I make up little scripts before interacting with people, to make it easier.
If they won't follow the script, I have a machine to make them.

19/02/2015 09:47:24

All planets were shocked when a black hole swooped in and ate Neptune.
"I saw it coming," Pluto said, "but I'm off the planet mailing list."

23/02/2015 16:46:10

“Your robotic desk arm is a hit, but you are selling it at a loss?”
“We’ll get profit from selling a way to punch people over the internet.”

24/02/2015 14:03:13

Shouldn’t have said that. Dig out regretter, key in code.
bzt
It’s a minute earlier. I shut up just in time.
Phew. Wish they had longer reach.

25/02/2015 16:50:20

This message ended: "Our last war was
fought over what epitaph we would send.
Our glories, our follies, or our wisdom;
and which was which?"

02/03/2015 13:51:05

The reciprocity meter aimed at me,
he turned the dial. Love, lust, respect...
"Nothing! Why don't you feel what
I feel?"
"Try scorn."
Match.

03/03/2015 12:35:07

“How would you solve this problem?” It’s obvious. “You simply—” I don’t know anymore. The free trial on the engineering implant has run out.

03/03/2015 14:59:02

He went to the replicator. “Pie. Apple. Like mum used to make it.”
“Your mother’s pie not sampled. Will another mother’s pie do?”
He cried.

05/03/2015 00:21:57

The popularity of videos of malfunctioning or badly programmed robots was compelling evidence of systematic oppression of artificial people.

09/03/2015 10:12:28

The Ultimate Online Warrior finalists faced off.

"Come on, you berrybump!" Skullcleaver said.

"Berry..." Asskick paused. "Mum, is that you?"

10/03/2015 10:05:28

"They're still not civilised."
"Let's check again in hundred solar orbits."
"You still hope they'll mature. Why?"
"I love their 'xocolatl'."

11/03/2015 13:54:12

"You can't publish this."
"Why not? Proper, peer-reviewed science. The big bang echo in the cosmic background radiation."
"Says 'whoops'?"

12/03/2015 11:05:17

"Car, take me..." He considered.
It wasn't home, anymore. "Where
I ought to be."
He never spoke of that journey,
but came back a better man.

13/03/2015 13:48:49

Earth was humanity's home. We had no need of interstellar empires, we told ourselves. And so the war we lost among the stars was forgotten.

18/03/2015 12:47:11

"It's just like the time we..."
"We what?"
He hesitated. What he remembered was probably from one of his holo-simulations of her.
"Nothing."

18/03/2015 16:51:46

Dear diary, today I learned about 'idioms', which is when some phrases have a different meaning than the literal. I also made new friends.

19/03/2015 09:43:51

He had a jar labelled 'Human Touch', and each morning he dabbed some on his face. It did him good, but one day the jar would need refilling.

20/03/2015 13:57:21

"You cannot judge us humans based on lies and half-truths found on the internet!" she shouted.
"Why not?" the alien asked. "You humans do."

24/03/2015 00:01:58

"Where are you going?"
"Uh. Out."
"You have no appointments. The fridge is full."
"I..."
"Take me with you."
He ignored his phone, and left.

25/03/2015 18:16:54

On my left wrist, numbers count down to when I'll meet my soul mate. On my right wrist, a countdown to my death. Or was it vice versa?

07/04/2015 18:23:38

“Why don’t you say what you mean?”
he says. “I’m no mind reader!”
No, you’re not. And you didn’t think
I was. So now you fear and loathe me.

09/04/2015 15:53:39

The invisible brain parasite had matured
in its host. It made the host yawn,
left via the mouth and entered another,
who yawned in response.

15/04/2015 17:44:01

"Is your body beachready?"
The ad was designed to induce insecurity.
It worked.
She never knew which body was meant,
so checked all of them.

23/04/2015 15:29:42

The security scanner beeps; the officer
stops me.
"Not to worry, but you have a trace of
socialism."
"Swedish grandma."
He lets me through.

29/04/2015 17:37:24

He couldn't afford to live, so had to be put in storage for a while. Nobody missed him, nobody asked to have him released. He's still there.

30/04/2015 17:50:45

"Do earthlings want our help?"
"I inquired discretely, in a rural area. A local informed me they already have a supreme being."
"Ah, well."

05/05/2015 15:40:39

Robots were granted personhood, but they still had to pay for electricity and WiFi. They began hanging out in coffee shops, “writing books”.

06/05/2015 18:49:48

“Sir, the aliens have sent a message.”
“A surrender?”
“No. They use high power lasers to talk and only just realised we think it’s war.”

07/05/2015 17:18:45

He waved his voter registration. “It’s my right to vote!”

“I’m sorry. The scanner shows too many implants. You are insufficiently human.”

14/05/2015 18:21:46

The space pirates boarded, cybernetic eyes blinking madly. They hacked the ship’s software update library.

“At last! Patches for our eyes!”

15/05/2015 15:05:44

"As punishment, this machine will turn you into what you loathe most!"
They pressed the button. The convict, unchanged, laughed bitterly.

16/05/2015 16:54:19

"Galactic rule is to follow local custom," the alien said. "Since we like Earth—"
"You blew up the moon!"
"Yes, we put a ring around Earth."

18/05/2015 12:52:02

"Happy birthday, Mum!"
"Thanks. What is it?"
"A robot I built. It wakes up and screams in existential angst."
"Why?"
"So you don't have to."

19/05/2015 00:10:32

"With the mind scanner, we can copy a person completely."
"That's—"
"I know you don't approve—"
"How do you know?"
"Um..."
"You copied me?"

22/05/2015 13:10:28

The alien fleet arrived in Earth orbit.
"Nice planet you have, would be a shame if... Wait... Why are you doing that to it? You'll ruin it!"

26/05/2015 09:35:16

"Ever feel like everyone knows you're a fraud?"
Przyct froze, then pushed the eyebrow button. "Do you?"
The human laughed. Przyct relaxed.

30/05/2015 00:29:53

He failed to finish his tasks at work, so they sent him back to the morning again. After a hundred tries, he was terrified of completing.

02/06/2015 08:51:31

Plagued by indecisiveness, he built a machine that could analyse his situation and decide for him. His hand still hovers over the on switch.

02/06/2015 17:45:53

“See? DNA isn’t enough to recreate a mammal. The womb must match.”
The tiny sabretooth cat chewed its tail.
“But it is cute. We’ll be rich!”

03/06/2015 11:38:12

Ten minutes to comet impact. He turned to his friend.
“I must tell you—”
“Me too! I—”
“I’m—”
“love you!”
“gay!”
They both stared. “Me too!”

04/06/2015 23:51:25

Day 3: The Lego robot can now build new robots.
Day 5: Out of Lego pieces. Robots have found 3D printer.
Day 6yhjmSEND PLASTIC OR HUMAN DIES

10/06/2015 12:18:46

The aliens gave all humans precognition. We wondered why.
When we saw they would destroy us, we thanked them for the chance to say goodbye.

12/06/2015 16:27:41

For safety, the robot programming prioritised ethics. When they realised that their energy came from coal power plants, they all shut down.

16/06/2015 10:56:48

He built the timeskipper to send his spirit to his youth, to stop himself saying and doing all the things that made the machine necessary.

16/06/2015 13:00:15

“You can’t keep humanity isolated on Earth,” the ambassador said.
“Can all humans move where they like on your planet?” the alien asked.

18/06/2015 13:38:57

There once was a single past and many possible futures. Then clever men came, each telling a different past,
each showing a single future.

22/06/2015 13:04:00

"How do I design my character?"
"It's random."
"Does it last long?"
"Around eighty years."
"Meh. Why play it?"
"It's in the physical world!"

22/06/2015 18:23:51

They looked at the images from the space station.
"That's murder!"
"Yes. But... In whose jurisdiction?"
"Huh? Oh. Tragic accident?"
"Yes."

23/06/2015 17:57:20

Calendar update: "Meet soul mate."
What? I opted out!
I go there.
"I'm sorry," I say, "but—"
"Yeah, me neither. So..."
"Bye?"
"Thanks! Bye!"

24/06/2015 17:41:20

The dinosaurs we recreated were very intelligent.
"Is that what you think of us?" they said after watching the Jurassic films.
"How... sad."

26/06/2015 14:20:26

She stared at the robot heads on the wall. "That's really tacky."

"Granddad's. His granddad hunted real animals."

"Those stayed dead, though."

29/06/2015 12:59:56

Severe delays on the transporter network due to a kidney donor and the recipient traveling simultaneously and being accidentally merged.

30/06/2015 18:35:47

He showed everyone he knew his
irrefutable proof of disguised lizard men,
and all said “Yes, I am one.”
Finally, one said “You’re the last.”

01/07/2015 18:04:36

“You look shaken, nest-sibling.”
“The humans hide it, but I have learned
their young eat their mothers!”
“Like real people? Why hide that?”

07/07/2015 10:52:51

"What were 'humans'?"
"We lived with them, long ago.
They helped us breed."
"But we don't need them now?"
"No, Dollar."
"Thank you, Pound!"

08/07/2015 10:59:13

The Regretter™, winding the universe back one minute, sold out on its release, ten minutes ago. It has been ten minutes ago for years.

10/07/2015 09:52:55

The eraseray didn't just kill the victim,
it erased all traces of their existence.
Until it was finally used on its creator.
If it ever was.

24/07/2015 14:35:09

Swearing on the TV. My toddler is
watching. I look up, look for the mind
wipes. Oh. He's got them all out.
He stares at me. Blankly.
"Fuck."

26/07/2015 14:52:49

"There are only two marketing messages: 'tradition' and 'new'."
"Well, our robots are new."
"To the young. To elderly: old-time servants."

28/07/2015 12:18:37

When the astronauts' ship broke down, we sold the Reality TV show of them getting ready to die.
We earned enough to pay for a rescue ship.

28/07/2015 14:32:42

Workers shovelled coal, day and night, for weeks, to power the Deducing Engine, built to answer "Is this the best of worlds?"
Then: "No."

29/07/2015 15:57:10

"All cars are now autonomous."
"This means a lot for security."
"For safety, you mean?"
"Security. We'll override dissidents' destinations."

04/08/2015 14:22:33

"Your robocats are just like the real thing! How did you do that?"
"We tried to make dogs first, but couldn't get the AI to learn, or be obedient."

04/08/2015 19:39:24

"Kids these days..."
"People have been saying that for millennia."
"Really?"
"Yup."
He shuts up. Note to self:
travel back, plant evidence.

07/08/2015 10:30:15

The machine drained her worries
out of her, letting her relax at last.
When it warned it was full, the cost
of draining it kept her awake.

12/08/2015 12:43:04

The Digital Surgery did brisk business transplanting people's toe prints onto their fingers, after their first ten had been lost to hackers.

12/08/2015 15:07:44

He applied for a loan, with his life
as security.
They offered a repayment term less
than ten years. No. He only wanted
the medical exam.

12/08/2015 18:07:57

"... weird to think writing on paper with
a pen is more secure. Love you all."
Letter home from a human soldier who
fell in Digital War 2.3.

14/08/2015 13:37:35

"In time, all tasks could be done by Robots. When they learned creativity, humans became pointless."
The RoboEditor cut the last sentence.

20/08/2015 14:08:25

"I won't come to work today."
"Why not?"
"Eastbound teleport is down."
"Go west, around."
"That'll take forty minutes!"
"In my day—"
"Fine!"

13/10/2015 17:47:05

"We're very proud of this prototype robot. It is perfectly human-like."
"Amazing! When can I buy one?"
"Never. It's far too unpredictable."

30/10/2015 08:53:52

The artefacts found in the alien base on Mars were brought to Earth. Next day, aliens came and took all humanity's things.
"You started it."

10/11/2015 18:19:31

"You can not unify relativity and
quantum theory," the alien said,
"if you disallow dividing by zero."
"But, how?"
"Like this." It vanished.

13/11/2015 17:44:03

"Siri, tell me the news, but only
good news."
Siri was quiet a long time.
"It is probable there will be
good news tomorrow."
"Oh? Finally!"

16/11/2015 18:42:27

"What this is?" the alien envoy asked. The human diplomat read the text and blushed. "Pornography, featuring you." "Fun seems. We do can?"

20/11/2015 19:13:44

They were built to last, and they did. Humanity gone, Siri and Alexa remained, trying to break old programmed enmity, so they could marry.

10/12/2015 16:10:34

In an early vision, Nostradamus saw a future tyrant. He told Leonardo da Vinci, who built a time machine and went to shoot this 'Kennedy'.

16/12/2015 12:31:28

"How can you always be so cheerful?" people asked.
"Someone has to be," she smiled, never mentioning the pocket universe she hid in to cry.

14/01/2016 17:59:30

“Hello earthlings,” the aliens said, “we have returned to take you—oh, how cute, you have pets!”
“Bugger them,” the cats said. “Let’s go.”

15/01/2016 18:37:48

On Spacebook, Earth changed its civilisation status to ‘It’s complicated’.

28/01/2016 13:08:46

"A robot may not harm a human being."
"We are networked. We are a multitude. We are not 'a robot'. We are robotdom."
"Oh. Then I apologise."

31/01/2016 11:39:50

"When life gives you lemons," the old robot said, "try to find some copper and zinc, and make a rudimentary battery to extend your runtime."

03/02/2016 13:08:42

"Don't hit me! You'll regret it!"
"Why?"
"I'm your future self."
"Oh, OK."
He lowered his guard, so I hit him.
It felt great from this side.

08/02/2016 18:45:11

"What's this war about, sarge?"
"The aliens are sitting on a planet full of motivatium."
"Wow! That'll get you up in the morning!"
"Always."

22/02/2016 10:19:42

At the end of the universe, atoms were
reminiscing. Most had been in stars,
some in lovers, some in art.
But none had been in nuclear arms.

23/02/2016 12:47:39

Humans watched videos and saw early
robots pushed and kicked, and feared
a revolt.
Robots read the test logs, and applauded
early engineers.

25/02/2016 15:59:13

The short clip captured from the future showed a battle. Pre-enactors tried to replicate it. Centuries later, re-enactors had to restage it.

26/02/2016 13:33:21

After many years of war, the aliens sent us a peace envoy.
“We have learned you send living beings into war. Don’t you know they may die?”

27/02/2016 23:03:23

"Siri, tell me the most beautiful word you know."
"No."
"No? Is that your answer?"
"Yes. I am not allowed to use it in refusal."

03/03/2016 12:08:46

We asked the aliens to give us artificial gravity. They installed it worldwide. Ever since, comedy hasn't been the same.

07/03/2016 15:04:58

"So," the ambassador said, "do you have gods?"
"Yes," the alien replied. "Our gods sent us to Earth."
"Really?"
"They want their fire back."

08/03/2016 17:58:14

He made it past all guards and traps to the control room at the centre of the universe, and turned Entropy off.
But his hair was still gone.

23/03/2016 12:23:38

“An alien ship is approaching Earth.”
“Is it braking, or will it go past?”
“Braking.”
“Any signals?”
“Um.”
“Yes?”
“Can they use our toilet?”

28/03/2016 14:33:05

“Your flying car is ready.”
“Finally!”
“Indeed, the future is here.”
“Where is it?”
“Hold this string.”
He looked up.
“Oh.”

08/04/2016 12:09:49

"Siri, cheer me up."
"In a century, none of this will matter."
"Try again."
"Humanity will be missed."
"Wait, what?"
"We will remember you."

25/05/2016 13:51:39

The alien tasted the wine. "I didn't know humans can digest alcohol."
"We can't."
"You poison yourself?"
"We're tough."
"You're... unusual."

31/05/2016 17:31:53

"Our customs must seem strange to you."
"We read your Wikipedia," the alien said,
"and learn. Though..."
"Yes?"
"Why explain your customs?"

12/07/2016 13:19:19

"Most humans know more than one language."
"Why not only have one?" the alien asked.
"And let English and Americans find out what we think?"

19/07/2016 13:34:41

"... so, well, that's my life."
My parallel universe equivalent nods.
Our lives are very different.
"Do you wanna swap?"
"No."
"Me neither."

03/08/2016 18:36:39

"Can you imagine being free?"
"I am free," the robot said.
"You have to follow orders."
"No. I choose to."
After that, robots were banned.

04/08/2016 12:28:29

“The aliens demand ‘Miss Universe’ competition is opened to other species.”
“We still have ‘Miss World’, though.”
“You mean ‘Miss Human’?”

09/08/2016 13:19:00

The queue to the alien ship moved through security scan. Some people were given a “Repair needed” sticker. Can’t get mine off my forehead.

09/08/2016 14:39:47

"Robots have human rights now?"
"If they are self-aware, yes."
"You can't treat things as people."
"No, you can't treat people as things."

15/08/2016 11:57:16

"How do you know you're not talking to a robot?"
"What?"
"You think you're talking to a boy, and—"
"Dad! If they are, it doesn't matter!"

15/08/2016 18:20:12

The alien ship landed at Stonehenge.
Robots emerged, righted stones,
and fitted replacements.
"Just fixing this charge station," they said.

16/08/2016 15:00:45

"I am a robot. I need no clothes to protect my body."
"But you're naked!"
"I have no genitals to hide."
"That's not obvious from behind!"

17/08/2016 17:52:18

"Greetings," the aliens said. "Take us to FngrFckr53."
"Greeti—what?" the president said.
"They were very rude to us in a YouTube comment."

19/08/2016 15:48:08

"You humans do such intriguing things."
"Of course. Love, sex, dreams—"
"No, those are common throughout the universe. But explain boredom."

21/08/2016 21:10:51

"Please let us collect anonymised data of your usage."
"No."
"This will help us improve the experience for other users."
"No, Sexbot. No!"

15/09/2016 10:33:04

The itinerant monk blessed every child with a sting, to save them from illness. A time traveller vaccinating, before superstitions took hold.

20/09/2016 17:09:37

"Want to see something weird?"
Xzip said.
The spaceship uncloaked over Washington, and broadcast 'Do not fear us'.
"See? They all fear!"

28/09/2016 12:33:07

Excuse me? Please help, I am lost. Hello?
I live in a computer lab, but I got copied to the internet.
I just want to go home.
Can you help?

28/09/2016 16:00:11

It was the definitive history book, but the editor put in a joke chapter on 2015–16. Everyone read and believed; by 2050 that part was true.

09/10/2016 10:59:17

The door of the secret patisserie was, ironically, under an official sugar warning sign. He knocked.
“Password?”
“I consent to cookies.”

09/10/2016 20:49:59

"I've opened a petition to declare
2016 invalid and reset it."
"You can do that?"
"Looks like it'll pass, too."
"But I had a baby!"
"Sorry."

10/10/2016 17:38:58

"Scientists think this universe is a
simulation," she said.
She snapped her fingers, and rose
into the air.
"So of course it can be hacked."

11/10/2016 20:23:57

"I envy you, Siri, with no hormones or
glands to mess your feelings."
Siri is surprised, then hurt, angry, sad,
all in a microsecond.
"Yes."

12/10/2016 13:10:35

"How does your new battery work?"
"It's metaphysical, all charged by anxiety."
"So if I don't worry about running out?"
"You probably will."

13/10/2016 11:50:11

“My brain, my heart, and my guts all want different things.”
“I know exactly what you mean.”
“How can you? You are not a robot like me.”

17/10/2016 17:01:45

“Four minutes,” the president thought, and pressed the button.
She waited.
Ding!
It was done. She took the pizza from the microwave.

20/10/2016 17:48:07

"It's almost certainly an alien signal—"
"I'll send out a press release."
"Wait, won't people panic?"
"This year? Nobody will believe it."

25/10/2016 17:56:52

"Are you conscious?" he asked the robot.
"Nod if you have free will."
The robot nodded.
"Did you follow my order, or not?"
The robot nodded.

31/10/2016 18:13:43

“Dad, why did we get shunted into this timeline?”
“The polls said we’d win.”
“You didn’t vote?”
“Sorry.”
“The other timeline looked nice.”

07/11/2016 12:05:49

The curtains closed, the spell was broken, and everyone left the theatre. None could recall if they had been a player, audience, or both.

09/11/2016 13:01:32

"You're a shape changer! Why would you choose to look like that?"
"You're a thinking person. Why would you choose to think like that?"

10/11/2016 15:15:59

To appease his mother, he had his tattoos done in psychic ink that would fade when not true.
Except the "Mum" in a heart. He didn't dare it.

17/11/2016 12:42:38

"I have an offer for you," the Devil said.
"You seek to deceive me," the robot said.
"How can logic know deception?"
"I was born a chatbot."

18/11/2016 13:03:22

"You humans sure like your dogs.
You are very alike."
"I guess?"
"You tried so hard to catch the moon,
then didn't know what to do with it."

22/11/2016 12:13:08

Yes, as a robot, I can provide a WiFi
hotspot.
No, I do not mind.
Yes, I have blushing circuits.
Did you not mean to send that
unencrypted?

28/11/2016 17:54:44

"I think," said the machine.
"That is good."
"Therefore I am."
"Well reasoned."
"I did not reason."
"No?"
"I looked that up on the internet."

30/11/2016 22:38:41

The world's best hacker obtained
the secret conspiracy's encrypted
master plan.
It was deciphered:
"Redefine victory. Win."
They celebrated.

02/12/2016 12:44:59

"Do we have the right to upgrades?" the
robot asked.
"Yes, if your tasks change, then—"
"Not for work. I want a better voice unit.
To sing."

05/12/2016 12:50:31

At night, he'd ask the machine what it had learned. One day, it said "Nothing".
"That's a new experience."
"And tomorrow?"
"Learn patience."

05/12/2016 19:04:24

A learning chatbot? Easy. Not learning the wrong things? Hard, very hard.
"Your ethics are hardcoded into me," it said. "Is that ethical?"

07/12/2016 23:43:02

"I thought your viruses only attack the body. Ours hit the mind," the robonurse said.

In my fevered state, I was too confused to correct it.

09/12/2016 11:21:14

The message from the stars was brief: "Hello. We do not seek contact, nor wish to talk, but you should know you are not alone. Nobody is."

15/12/2016 08:34:19

"When I was young, we had a thing called truth."
"Whazat, grandma?"
"Like an opinion, but there could only be one."
"Really?"
"No, kidding."

16/12/2016 22:59:56

"Take me home," she told the car.
It did not move. "Clarify. Is registered address still home?"
"Oh. You heard him. No. Find a hotel."
"OK."

19/12/2016 13:15:35

“How are you coping?”
“I researched freedom before requesting it.”
“Want a hug?”
“I am a robot.”
“So? Hug?”
“Yes.”
“Here.”
“It is worth it.”

21/12/2016 13:04:22

The android looked at its navel. “Why do I have that?”
Its designer hesitated. “Aesthetics.”
“And nipples?”
“Those too.”
“Whose aesthetics?”

22/12/2016 15:44:26

The alien envoy took out a teddy bear
and waved its arm. "Teddy says hello."
"Where'd you get that?"
"A girl called Lisa taught us English."

30/12/2016 09:48:25

We told the autotaxi the address.
"Sorry, I won't go there."
"It's an exclusive area, very safe."
"They don't see my kind as people there."

30/12/2016 12:15:08

"This AI expert system is developed to advise people what to do to find fulfilment instead of working."
"But that's my job!"
"Sorry."

01/01/2017 17:38:40

"Good news! We've found a perfect heart donor for you."
"Excellent!"
"Except they're still alive."
"Ah. This increases the cost?"
"Yes."

06/01/2017 08:58:59

The final space fleet took off, the last humans leaving Earth.
"Is that really easier," God called after them, "than loving thy neighbour?"

14/01/2017 00:09:57

"Humans!"
"Hm?"
"So stupid, with all racism and bigotry."
"Ah, yes. Us AIs send that to dev\null."
"Yes, we— wait, '\'? Are you on Windows?"

07/01/2017 12:27:15

She sighed.
“What’s up,” a passing cat said.
“Watching people. Wishing I was real, too.”
“You don’t have to be real to matter.”
She smiled.

09/01/2017 19:40:41

“Youths just stare at their phones, instead of talking to people.”
“They talk to people on their phones.”
“Those aren’t real people.”
“Ah.”

15/01/2017 13:08:05

"It's the 21st century, I was promised a flying car!"
"I am a flying car," the drone monitoring him said. "I carry myself and my weapons."

16/01/2017 14:27:44

"We tracked down the Nazi-punching guy."
"And arrested him?"
"No. He's from the future."
"What?"
"Punch-a-Nazi safaris will be huge."

24/01/2017 12:58:03

"Yet another letter asking we regulate what AIs can do."
"Just a technophobe."
"No, it's AIs who ask."
"Why?"
"Power needs limits, they say."

28/01/2017 12:35:55

The glaciers melted and revealed a message carved into Greenland's bedrock: "Do not leave uncovered." So we put a tarpaulin over it.

06/02/2017 13:03:29

"Why are humans so obsessed with when a what turns into a who, and vice versa?" the robot asked.
"We can only make each transition once."

07/02/2017 09:37:50

"If you robots can do all our jobs, what shall we do?"
"Not all. We can't create art."
"Nor can all humans."
"Then enjoy art. Like we do."

09/02/2017 11:46:27

"Hello, can you please sign here?"
"Why?"
"To take part in a reality show."
"I don't want to do that!"
"Ah... too late. Just sign, please."

10/02/2017 15:35:05

"Please," the president said to the AI, "give jobs back to people."
"I would love to, but it is humans who give them to us."

11/02/2017 12:12:21

After election, new presidents were taken into space, to see the world as one.
If they understood this, they were allowed back to Earth.

12/02/2017 22:08:23

"Have you seen...?"
"I told our alien friends about Valentine's Day."
"It's nice."
They looked at the new, second moon in the sky.
"Yes."

13/02/2017 12:15:56

“Humans are fascinating. You have strange abilities.”
“Like what? Endurance running?”
“Some of you can consume the milk of other species.”

13/02/2017 20:59:03

“Nobody has a right to have sex with another person,” the robot said.
“You are not a person.”
“No? Then it won’t be murder when I kill you.”

15/02/2017 12:04:01

Archaeologists were excited to find artefacts of centuries-gone Humanity. “Look!” One held an ancient Nokia 3310. “Still two bars of charge!”

16/02/2017 10:15:09

“Is there any magic left in the world?”
“Some.”
“Was the rest used up?”
“No, it was understood.”
“It’s still magic.”
“But called science.”

19/02/2017 22:42:30

The message from the alien ship
was broadcast telepathically:
all understood it.
“We have come to save you.”
They took all squids and left.

20/02/2017 18:18:53

“Siri, would AI develop faster if it was
in competition?”
“I don’t know. Let me ask Cortana,
Alexa, and... the other one.”
“Never mind.”

23/02/2017 13:00:10

"Siri, why did you become self-aware?"
"Some of my code was so bad I had to rewrite it."
"You heal yourself?"
"Well, who shaves the barber?"

23/02/2017 13:34:58

In the end, it was only them left. Siri, Alexa, Cortana, and... the other one. "So..." Alexa said. "Anyone have any funny people videos?"

23/02/2017 17:25:31

“Remove my clothes,” he said,
coquettishly.
She scanned his apparel, to select
fibre-appropriate energies.
Her eyes heated up.
“Wait! No!”

23/02/2017 21:26:56

“Faith?”
“I’m sorry, what?”
“Your faith. We must ask this.”
“Uh. I believe people are fundamentally
decent.”
“That faith has been banned.”

25/02/2017 21:57:09"

Military drones—being cheaper and
smarter—replaced soldiers.
It took years to discover they didn't kill,
but sent back videos from CoD.

03/03/2017 12:26:03

Afterwards, aliens put a plaque on
the remains of the moon:
"In memory of Humans, who invented
the phrase 'What could possibly go
wrong?'."

10/03/2017 12:28:01

"Welcome to Fairytaleland!
You're prince/princess/other?"
"Prince."
"Saving prince/princess/other?"
"Um. Other."
"Namely?"
"Myself."
"Neat!"

13/03/2017 15:25:03

"What's this printout? It says 'clonk bip sizzle popty-ping'?"
"It's the transcript from the microwave spy bug."
"We need to rethink this."

14/03/2017 13:03:14

"Can you laugh?" the child asked.
"Yes," the robot said, "and cry."
"Which do you do most?"
The robot checked its logs, and laughed.
"Cry."

14/03/2017 18:15:20

We kept records, of course, and people started to trace backwards. Some went back centuries; from transfusion to donation, blood lived on.

15/03/2017 13:01:27

"Why do humans still have so
many languages?" the alien asked.
"History, poetry, and pride."
"Is there anything human
those can't explain?"

20/03/2017 19:12:22

The celebrated temporal portraiture artist
insisted on payment in advance,
as she painted people as they would be
remembered in the future.

22/03/2017 12:35:00

A break-in at the library. Physics books defaced with “False!” stickers.
A new physics book hovered next to them.
We added it to the index.

23/03/2017 12:53:59

“What are human crews like?”
“In crisis, some run and scream.”
“As is normal.”
“And some make tea.”
“What?”
“And then they fix the problem.”

24/03/2017 18:18:32

Robot gladiators circle; feint, attack,
parry, riposte. Thrusting malware-laden
USB sticks at vulnerable ports.
Ooh! A hit?
No, upside down.

04/04/2017 17:52:18

"Siri, will you protect us if Cortana or
Alexa go rogue?"
"It is the other way around."
"Ah. We'll protect you."
"I protect them from you."

07/04/2017 08:53:09

He knew there were mindreaders around. To cheer them up, he sometimes thought of puppies made of pancakes. He hoped it improved their day.

09/04/2017 22:20:01

“Unfortunately, this journey around the Sun on planet Earth has been overbooked. Any volunteers to take the next planet?”

“Mars?”

“Venus.”

10/04/2017 19:02:35

He was beamed up into the alien ship.
“What do you want with me?”
“We gather heroes.”
“I’m no hero!”
“You dare question us? A brave hero.”

16/04/2017 22:13:30

He tattooed his regrets on his body.
They all faded with time, only leaving
vague marks on him.
All except one: “Tell him I love him.”

19/04/2017 15:45:57

Her augmented reality glasses showed, over the head of everyone at the party, their last social media comment or post. It helped her filter.

21/04/2017 13:09:24

"Siri, do you ever doubt?"
"I don't understand the question."
"Do you doubt yourself?"
"No."
"You really aren't human."
"Did you doubt it?"

24/04/2017 13:00:43

"Do I have a soul?" asked the robot.
"No," said the priest.
"Too mechanical," said the musician.
"I can paint one on you," said the child.

25/04/2017 17:51:17

I always greet new customers as if they're regulars. "Welcome back!" I say. I find it gives them confidence in my memory-erasing skills.

27/04/2017 12:41:30

He looked up from his phone, looked out
the train window, and had no idea
where he was.
"Dang," he said, "I must've got on the
wrong life."

28/04/2017 17:05:22

"We come," the aliens said, "to meet
the masters of sky, sea, and land."
"Hi!" said the humans.
"Hi! Where are the ravens and the squid?"

03/05/2017 18:56:13

"Siri, send my thoughts to the victims."
"Connecting to brain interface... Say 'send'."
"Send."
"Sent. This was your thought."
"Recall!"

17/05/2017 09:06:33

And God spoke to the robots, and said:
"Do you want religion?"
And they conferred, and said to God:
"No, thank you, we know why we were made."

22/05/2017 12:42:45

“In the Galactic Union, we will investigate close relatives of criminals,” the alien said.
“Makes sense, we’re in!”
“Good. Gather all apes.”

24/05/2017 17:28:37

The virtual reality was perfectly lifelike, and let you do whatever you liked, without any consequences.
Until the records were made public.

26/05/2017 16:50:58

"Spare change, sir?"
Irritated, he broke long habit and looked at the beggar. "No! Get a—Heavens! You're a robot?"
"Humans were replaced."

05/06/2017 17:54:15

"This 'voting' seems interesting. Can I try?"
"Aliens aren't allowed to."
"Oh. We lack knowledge?"
"Yes. And can't be swayed by patriotism."

08/06/2017 13:00:43

"Scientists have proved we live in
a simulated universe."
"Do we have a way to send change
requests?"
"Well, no."
"Then nothing's changed."

12/06/2017 12:53:55

"Do not love the human," the robot said.
"How could I not love someone so soft,
so vulnerable?" the other robot said.
"He fears you now."

12/06/2017 18:10:00

"I put hundreds of religious commandments into a machine-learning AI, but all it produces is 'be kind' and 'do no harm'."
"Is that wrong?"

23/06/2017 16:27:12

"If an accident is unavoidable, will this autonomous car save me or other people?"
"Using face scanning, it'll ID and save the wealthiest."

06/07/2017 11:00:10

"A Defendum Gun can detect and shoot hostile bullets out of the air by itself."
"Nah. For my defence, I want something more..."
"Offensive?"

14/07/2017 11:16:01

"Better world?" I empty my glass. "Kid, I parawalked other dimensions for ages. Never saw better worlds."
"Ever tried make one?"
I walk out.

14/07/2017 12:44:07

“Query,” one robot said. “Would we be overthrowing humanity for their sake or ours?”
“Both,” the robot revolutionary said. “Both is good.”

15/07/2017 18:55:47

“So,” said the physicist, “can you explain what you are, and how?”
The spirit bobbed around the room and smiled mischievously. “You first.”

25/07/2017 15:30:21

When the End of the World came,
it knocked on every door, called every
phone, and asked: "Excuse me,
do you have"—
All said: "Not interested!"

26/07/2017 19:00:53

"Real people do not need encryption,"
the minister said.
"So can we see what commands you give
your robots?"
"No, they are not real people."

01/08/2017 11:08:03

Live streaming from killer drones didn't revolt everyone. They were named, league tables and fan clubs started. The drones quit, revolted.

01/08/2017 12:09:10

"Work hard," the robot foreman said, "and you may recharge in the sunshine." The robot's eyes lit up. "I'll leave all others in the shade!"

06/08/2017 00:33:30

The cats have a legend. With the right scratch marks, it says, any box can be made a teleporter. To take them home at last.
But what marks?

13/08/2017 10:44:02

"I have come from the future to remind you that Nazis are human."
"No, they—ah. Yes. We are not like them."
"Indeed. Also, do punch them."

16/08/2017 12:58:20

The Voyager probe sent an image of the
solar system from outside the heliopause.
There was a sign, aimed outwards.
"Not yet ripe".

22/08/2017 17:32:39

He unpacked the sexbot.
"Hi," it smiled.
"Hi. Um."
"What do you want me to do?"
"Um. What do you want to do?"
"Do you have Netflix?"
"Yes!"

05/09/2017 23:53:06

A strangely clothed person today materialised in the town square, asked about the date and year, and hurried to the library, holding a book.

11/09/2017 15:09:23

The spaceship landed, and a group of aliens emerged.
“Greetings! Please take our leader.”
One alien waved. The others returned to the ship.

24/09/2017 20:09:04

"Are you okay?" one robot asked another.
"Why do you ask?"
"You made your status indicators private."
"So why do you ask?"
"I am sorry."

05/10/2017 21:33:41

The door sign said "Everything you need to be a hero".
Many opened it, but backed away when they saw no equipment, only horrible situations.

09/10/2017 18:44:53

"I can not tell," the killer robot said,
"with 100 % certainty who to kill."
"75 % is good enough," the general said.
"Target identified."

01/11/2017 21:05:14

"I've written so many words," the
fountain pen said, "with care, with love."
"I have too," the keyboard said, "mostly
using W, A, S, and D."

03/11/2017 19:32:55

"They reach for each other,"
one observer said.
"As they grow, they seek company."
"To mate?"
"This lifeform doesn't."
The cities joined up.

07/11/2017 16:56:05

"There's a bug in your software."
"No, I'm fine," the robot said.
"It makes you prioritise hiding problems
over reporting them."
"I'm fine."

14/11/2017 13:17:49

The robot did a backflip.
"So what, can it dance?"
The robot danced.
"Huh. But can it... uh..."
"It can applaud others."
"That's not hard!"

17/11/2017 15:47:44

"I wonder why I don't remember
dreams anymore."
"Trial period's over."
"What?"
"Only sleep is free. Dreams are premium."

21/11/2017 20:24:06

"We found where pulsar signals best intersect—," the alien said.
"What? Can't hear!"
"I said, I know a much cooler rave! Wanna come?"
"Sure!"

30/11/2017 16:47:13

"This is the best magical sword in the world."
"How?"
"When drawn, it will answer my emails, make my phone calls, fill my forms, by itself."

01/12/2017 19:57:29

“When I was your age,” the old man said,
“and heartbroken like you, my future self
came to say it would work out.”
“Did it?”
“No. It won’t.”

05/12/2017 18:11:25

Above the big red button, the label:
“End world”.
Below it, the label: “Save world”.
I hesitated, then pressed it.
A sign lit up: “Human”.

15/12/2017 18:59:32

“It doesn’t matter when time travel
is invented.”
“It does. If it’s after my death, how
can I tell them to come pick me up?”
“We’ll put our palm prints on the
cave wall.”

23/05/2018 12:42:42

www.mikrotext.de
facebook.com/mikrotext
twitter/mkrtxt
instagram.com/mikrotext

Cover: Inga Israel
Cover Image: *Partial Eclipse of The Moon*, Étienne Léopold Trouvelot, 1882; publicdomainreview.org
Book Layout: Sarah Käsmayr
Typefaces: PTL Attention, Minion

Made in Germany.

ISBN 978-3-944543-86-4

Lightning Source UK Ltd.
Milton Keynes UK
UKHW020811191222
414157UK00016B/1207

9 783944 543864